Polly pocket ™

PollyWorld ™

Extreme Scavenger Hunt

Written by Pamela Jane
Illustrated by MADA Design, Inc.

© 2006 Mattel, Inc. and/or Origin Products Ltd.
The POLLY POCKET trademark is owned by Origin Products Ltd.
Other trademarks and trade dress are owned by Mattel, Inc. or
Origin Products Ltd. Manufactured under license from Mattel, Inc.
First Edition.
All Rights Reserved.

Manufactured and printed in the United States of America.
ISBN-13: 978-0-696-23188-9
ISBN-10: 0-696-23188-3

We welcome your comments and suggestions.
Write to us at: Meredith Books, Children's Books,
1716 Locust St., Des Moines, IA 50309-3023.
Visit us online at: meredithbooks.com

Meredith® Books
Des Moines, Iowa

D0131582

"What's the big secret, Polly?" asks Shani.

"This weekend is the grand opening of PollyWorld!" exclaims Polly. "Our class will be competing in contests on TV! Our final challenge is to conquer PollyWhirl, the biggest, fastest roller coaster ever built!"

The girls jump up and down, cheering and shouting—all except Crissy.

No one notices that Crissy is quiet.

Polly and her pals arrive at PollyWorld. The girls gaze in awe at Polly's dazzling new theme park. Towering over everything is the PollyWhirl, the heart-poundingest roller coaster in the world.

Polly's class divides into three teams of five.
"Five is the perfect number," says Polly. "We can all be together!"
"Five friends forever!" says Lila.

"Everything is always so perfect for Polly," grumbles Beth. "But this time Team Beth is going to come out on top, skyrocketing me to number one popular girl at school!"

"The first team that completes all five competitions in any order is the winner," announces Miss Marklin, their teacher. "The first competition is Ride the Rapids—Upstream!"

Team Pocket races against the raging current.
"Move over for the winning team!" shouts Beth,
paddling frantically past Polly's raft.
Team Beth beats Team Pocket to the finish line!

Polly and her pals are soaked and laughing.
"That was fun, even if we didn't win," says Shani.
"Just wait until we tackle PollyWhirl," says Lea.
Crissy says nothing and tries to hide her worry.

The next challenge is to Stretch a
Licorice Whip Across America.
When Polly flashes a thumbs-up
sign, everyone takes a big bite.

On PollyWalk the girls make the panels light up to spell out their names.

"I always dreamed of seeing my name in lights!" says Lea.

"Time to play Fire a Cannon!" says Shani.
Polly and her pals put on bathing suits and
cannonball into a big pool.

"Next we rule PollyWhirl!" cries Lila.

Crissy stares wide-eyed up at the monster roller coaster as the others run off laughing and shouting.

"Wait!" Crissy calls after them. "I can't do it!"

"I'm afraid of tiny, little roller coasters," Crissy confesses. "And PollyWhirl is the biggest, fastest, heart-poundingest, lunch-losingest roller coaster in the world!"

Polly puts her arm around Crissy.
"No big," she says. "You don't
have to go on it."

Crissy's eyes fill with tears. "But . . .
we can't win if I don't."

"Making sure you're OK is more important than winning," says Lila.
All the girls agree.
"Come on, let's bounce back to the rapids ride," says Shani.

As they are leaving, they meet Beth and her friends.

"Well, if it isn't Team Pocket!" says Beth. "I hope you're not planning on winning, because we're about to finish our last challenge—the PollyWhirl!"

"Good luck, Beth," says Polly.
Team Pocket turns to go.
"Wait!" cries Crissy suddenly. "If Beth can handle PollyWhirl, so can I!"

"Are you sure?" asks Polly.

Crissy's heart is pounding, but she nods firmly. "Just promise that someone will hold my hand!"

The girls smile and join hands.

Polly and her pals pile into the coaster car.
"No fair!" says Beth. "We were here first.
Our car should go ahead of . . . ahhhhhhh!"
Beth shrieks as the roller coaster takes off
with a jolt.

PollyWhirl flies up and down hills, hurtles around corkscrews, and charges through loops.

"Are you OK, Crissy?" asks Polly, as both cars come to a stop.

"No," says Crissy. "Because Beth's team is about to beat us!"
The two teams run toward the finish line. At the last second, the third team suddenly appears and slides into first place, beating them both!

"Chillax, girls," says Polly. "Winning isn't everything. We're the best of friends and that's what counts."

Crissy grins. "Who's up for another ride on the biggest, fastest, MOST FUN roller coaster in the entire world?"

Meet Polly and her friends!

Polly

Lea

Shani

Crissy

polly pocket™

Lila